DR. MARBLES
& MARIANNE

DR. MARBLES & MARIANNE

— A ROMANCE —

NICKI JACKOWSKA

Harvester Press

First published in Great Britain in 1982 by

THE HARVESTER PRESS LIMITED
Publisher: John Spiers
16 Ship Street, Brighton, Sussex

Designed by Craig Dodd

British Library Cataloguing in Publication Data
Jackowska, Nicki
   Dr. Marbles and Marianne.
   I. Title
   823'.914[F]   PR6060.A18

   ISBN 0-7108-0490-3

Typeset in Andover by
Photobooks (Bristol) Limited
Printed in Great Britain by
Photobooks (Bristol) Limited

For Father
with love

Acknowledgements

Selections from 'Doctor Marbles and Marianne' have appeared in *Ambit* and *Kudos* magazines, as well as the anthology *Last Fly*.

DR. MARBLES & MARIANNE

RED, FOR MARRIAGES

And Marbles said, my laboratory is a
grove of fine sons who will talk in my
many voices and make a red hunting
chorus for me.

Between you and me and the moths and
the crickets and the goat, I want to go
home, said Marianne (seeing nothing
but red).

And slid from under his wing.

What! Leave this game of consequences
with its red faces and its grove of new
songs, said Marbles, leading her into
the red and brimming room where eyes
hovered and words dripped from the
walls.

A moth drowned in the wastepipe.
Marbles in his red shirt (one button
missing) computing unknown jungles,
lakes and groves, in moonlight

It is a red month, said Marianne.
I hunt at dawn in a grove of daughters,
silent as the knife that dips and
seeks the root.
And so she slept.

Over the hills, the ticking of one
heart; the grove of small trees
stained red, the sounding of names,
came and went in their dream. . . .

THE PROTAGONISTS

Doctor Marbles

He is a computer scientist, a judo black belt, and owns a castle in Scotland. He has a collection of hardware, software, swords, notebooks, containers (including laboratories) and people. Marianne is his prize specimen.

He is heavily built with a high forehead and not much hair. He is fastidious and dislikes undulations and curves. He plays chess. He has a friend who collects motor-bikes. His master plan or project is to freeze the universe into measurable proportions.

One of the ways to bring it under control, is to eliminate diversity. This he does by attempting to reduce the variety of species by cross-fertilisation into one strain.

Another way is to replace all organic things with inorganic ones. At the same time they will be reduced in size as they are translated from what they are into IN-FORMATION, and stored in great numbers in very small spaces, in computers.

He also dislikes the coloured shirts that Marianne keeps on buying for him.

Could be small and fair-haired. Not very robust.

She has a sister, also called Marianne, who once won a beauty contest at Butlins. Marianne admires her sister, and often thinks of her when in difficulty.

Marianne (the fair one) collects shoes, blouses, shawls, suspender belts and masks. She studies botany, and is particularly fond of the fifty-seven varieties of ice-cream. (Italian).

She met Marbles at a conference in Leeds. They were thrown together quite by accident on the afternoon off, when a number of scientists went for a walk together to explore the sights. She was there as a research assistant studying the psychology of scientists at conferences in an urban setting when removed from their natural habitat, with particular reference to off-duty behaviour.

Marbles and Marianne have no children, neither each other's or anyone else's. It could be that there is a causal relationship between this fact, and their subsequent behaviour.

On the other hand, there may not be.

DOCTOR MARBLES MEETS MARIANNE

God in his infinite wisdom turned over in bed and the sub-lunar insect-layer crouched in paralysis.

Doctor Marbles took out his eye (the one that was capable only of reflection and contained a sophisticated visual recording device) and diagnosed motor-failure of the nerve-channels. *Dementia praecox* among the lizard family.

He watched his opponent. In his laboratory, each party in the horny embrace (Marbles' insistence) fell to the floor panting. They're all the subjects of a gigantic hoax, he mumbled, sending forth his pronouncements upon fibrous indians and the scaly streets of golden-tongued california. Without however uttering a word. His companion had spread the luminous wings of childhood across the chalky walls of his laboratory.

Marbles was playing chess. He was losing.

His eye rested on the kingdom of the white queen.

The maintenance of buddhahood is no joke said his opponent, flashing a picture of himself assembling the motor-cycle which would carry him across the seven states of consciousness straight home to tea with his Aunt Alice.

He lost his sense of direction. Marbles greedily took the white knight.

Marbles' black socket was swallowing the thoughts of his friend. Its the end of the monster-merchants, Marbles said, worrying over the failure of his latest move to unite lizard and queen at one stroke.

He wondered how such a charlatan had ever been invited to the conference.

Marianne wandered along the borders of an old sluggish moon, painting the names of her ancestors, visitors, statues, gardeners, croquet-guests, pulling wings from fat bodies.

The crowd spoke, falling and spelling.

Marianne smelt winter on her breath.

I need a shot, she said, a root.

Holding her head between two hands, she felt the tide rising.

The stars fell. She was a child again, flung haphazard on the air.

Marbles, looking down the long end of his telescope, observed the phenomenon. A cloud moving, a dandelion clock, a ball of spun glass.

He took the negatives, shadows, after-images, chrysalides, that were Marianne, folded the specimen neatly into a large yellow handkerchief stained with tea. Born under scorpio, he couldn't avoid the dreadful beating of his own time-clock. Inside his pocket, Marianne's heart chimed at intervals to the tune of the low tide.

Pavements empty of ants. Webs hanging empty. Marbles' clean-up job stripped the city of subterranean sound.

Marbles mused on the sudden silence, an absence of crickets' legs, the sub-terrestrial chorus, laboratory underfoot. It was going to be difficult, replacing such reliable allies. He considered fitting the contents of toy-shops with computers, programmed into obedience. But that was just the point. It was no good consulting oracles if you knew the story in advance. A twin-iguana choice-mechanism?

His pocket was a large cave. Outside something short-circuited. Marbles had tripped over the corpse of a salamander and lay sprawled over the pavement, ticking madly.

It was unfortunate that he cut his forehead and needed his pocket handkerchief to mop the blood. Her flight into the world was a trauma of skin and cloth.

I've seen you somewhere before, said Marbles, staring up at her who was leaning against a tree trying to catch her breath which whistled through the space and sent buds flying.

He had a lonely worm's eye view of legs and a neat white triangle.

I have a colleague who knows a lot about motor-cycles, said Marbles. She nodded. Marianne's moon-map shifted a little towards mars. Scorpio rising? said Marianne.

Marbles creaked, thinking of the amphibian dark.

Well yes but under control, he assured her. And his hair flowed and his tail twitched in its tightly-woven knot.

I might try insecticides, he thought.

Are you of the faith? Marbles asked.

She pulled down her blouse to reveal a nipple high up under her arm.

Splendid, then you must see my laboratory, Marbles said. Dusting a cloud of expiring ants from his lapel, Marbles fixed both eyes on the same spot and watched the whirlpool form into Marianne's face.

Under that particular constellation, there was no hope of a union. But his ambition knew no limits. Even now, he was working on mechanisms for moving the stars. Not to mention destruction of that awful yawning chasm between scale and flesh, leaf and hide, bud and nipple, claw and foot, nail and . . . but the list was endless.

Milky and delightfully opaque after her descent, Marbles saw that he could safely leave his name-hunting until after tea. For Marianne would obviously be of no use to him until fed. He had a strong sense of paternity. As if the whole animal and plant kingdom did not occupy his nursery—a new offspring?

DOCTOR MARBLES' LABORATORY IN
FLIGHT: MARIANNE ATTENDING

Now there is understanding sweet as the earth.

Marianne speaks with the tongue of night.

Black spaces open wide in Marbles' skull. She is of the sisterhood. She belongs to skin-language. The hissing chorus of crystal and coloured contents like an open vertebra spilling the marrow. She is his daughter. . . .

No, I never did manage marriage, he said.

Your name is unusual, she said.

Marbles thought, I am a speck dancing inside my skull. I can hear music on the brink of its incarnation. I can hear all my intentions rattling like beads in there. My arabesque words in this quiet space, unfurnished, untenanted, write me into this room.

What if I stop dancing?

What if the speck shrinks to infinity?

What if she constructs my favourite dance-tunes inside my speck-skin, shrinking?

Shall I have the chance to know that I am Marbles?

What a lot of questions you ask, said Marianne. I am not a doctor. I am not a prophet. I am not a philosopher. I am not a theologian. I am not an expert. I am not a biologist. I am not a gynaecologist. I am not a wastepaper-basket for all your unsatisfied, unknown, unrealised, unheard-of propositions . . . and took off her shiny clothes, one by one, unpeeling rainbows.

Marbles sat panting.

The effort to stop himself dancing had exhausted him.

She opened a carton of neapolitan ice-cream, rubbing her thighs, and her legs slowly opened among his bubbling forest of glassy undergrowth.

I am not your ideal model, she said, but you may borrow me for the day.

Marbles' new experiment took twenty-four hours precisely.

TRANSFORMER: OF MARBLES

Grass over Marianne's foot. The extent of green.

Their journey took place within five hours of capture. She turned on the heating system and allowed Marbles to shed his overcoat, his jacket, his lambswool jumper and his stiff socks. Caught in an undertow, he approaches this particular green sea wondering what he is supposed to do, what there can possibly be to discover in this innocence. Such an absence of invitation. The tune of Marianne's breath as a humming, menacing, asking, questioning, unfolding, regretting. Marbles wants with all his accumulated, formulated, symbolic strength to return to base. To the charted uncertainty of his fibreglass lunation cycles. The man underneath catches sight of a dragonfly, is caught in a moth wing.

She is very large on the hill ahead of him, getting larger. His bones begin to creak, her dress seems a spreading cloud and he can't focus. Out of the corner of his eye the edge of her, uncertain. Darkness rears up between every blade, every step. Marianne's dress is an indigo waterfall, overhung with creepers; he takes the sting gladly feels her sweet juice turning to lead in his veins. Inside Marianne a flight to the sea, called moss, where dark damp secrets are poured into his ears and the ringing butterflies shed years of themselves.

Crackle of her clothes coming off like paper.

Rasp of the earth, out of breath, taking her.

Hiss of the fingers clawing at her belly. Red at the end of it for gods and blasphemy.

She lifted the soft white pillow and rolled him downhill. Head over heels upside down, rolling with Marianne pinned to his side like a sister, calling on the land to be still, asking forgiveness, licking the air, wishing she would be still and opaque and fuck him again until the songs came and the trees crashed into his ears. They landed somewhere between twilight and equinox, the sixth of august nineteen seventy-five. They landed on the same slope, Marianne's indigo dress floating above him like a dream remembered, Marianne's legs inside his head, her tongue in his throat, her hair searing his back. The dragonfly flickering in the corner of his eye.

It's too hot, said Marbles, I must rest.

Not far to the top, says Marianne.

MARIANNE TO KING PAWN

The scarred edge of the blackberry bush was the horizon. Marianne lay several skins later under the heel of the sky, tubes and testimonies flying from her flesh like a flock of startled seagulls. The scream of glass, the shriek of all the mistakes that led to the one final statement: I am alive, said Marianne, crushing the blood-berries to prove it. It appeared that Marbles hadn't thought much of his sample. It appeared that he had thought so little of his specimen that he had thrown her, apparatus and all, half the letters missing, at the side of a country road. In fact he had not even bothered to disguise the machinery of testing. He had been so careless that Marianne found it hard to believe that his laboratory could continue to breathe and function in such conditions. If he became so angry at the least resistance to conform, then surely half his glass-castle was now scattered over the english country-side like so much picnic litter. Not to mention the gases, human and otherwise, which were escaping into the pure crystal english air.

Marianne smoothed her crumpled thoughts and decided upon action, each breath irritated so many yards of rubber tubing, making a rustle like snakes in the grass. In fact stillness was impossible, such a labyrinth of delicacy encased her. She felt like a visitor to the hinterland. Every breath caused a whisper in the underworld, all the china vibrating to the movements of air.

Well it wasn't china. (She had been thinking of tea in the conference dining room). It was Marbles and his damned rubber and glass. How on earth had she been seduced into this crenellated forest? It was time she shed her intoxication with professors, along with their junkyards. Only Marbles she knew, had a computer. And it knew all about her. It sucked in all her hidden names right back to the year zero, and all her cellular history was spelled out in its brain. She remembered all the secrets she had yelled out at the heart of Marbles' glittering embrace, how many times she had called out in recognition of some phantom mirrored in the lenses of his spectacles. What treacherous acts she had performed as one delightful resin after another was inhaled, ingested, consumed, and delicacies of Marbles' culinary art were fed to her day after day as his hands worked on her flesh until she was a writhing atom on the tip of his supercharged finger.

She grew quite breathless thinking of it.

And the glass tree shivered and tinkled. She felt the palms of her hands sweating so that all the tubing began frosting over. It is time, said Marianne, to start where I am, and ceased climbing the endless staircases of her past ecstasies.

There was a tight steel helmet clamped to her head. So thin was it, that she had trouble finding the line where it joined her scalp. It had to be prized off, and her hands with their trailing glass ribbons felt cumbersome and not quite her own. There was also the uncomfortable sensation of the tubes banging and sliding across her face as she worked away at the helmet. She broke a couple of nails. She cursed her benefactor.

You will be expanded beyond measure, he

had said. You will know the stars. You will be restored to your rightful consciousness.

All Marianne could feel was a mortal chill from the damp autumn earth, and a mortal longing for a warm-blooded, mortal man with a bank account and a large bed to take her unto him.

The helmet moved up her skull a tenth of an inch and she felt it separate itself from her head right on the top. A tiny gap between steel and flesh. Her hands fluttered over the outside. Tiny nodules at intervals. Ragged ends of thin wire sticking out from some of them.

Electricity! she thought.

MARIANNE'S DREAM OF THE ODEON

I once had a lover made of the glass splinters of Christmas, the catatonic rhyming of trees under a slow vesuvious sky, the crystalline shreds at the ends of winter roads. I hung up my beaver coat in his hallway that smelt of liquorice and took off my shoes that were flung wide up under the beams like two black doves.

I once had a lover who wore well, like horse-chestnuts.

He gave me berries, one at a time, slowly.

He fed the matrimonial fire with just enough fine sticks for a fleeting pattern in the flames. He took off his clothes with the precision of ice forming under paleolithic cave-mouths.

I took off my blouse like a white sheath of silk that slid past my skin as though I never owned it.

Knowing only the laborious march of flame, cool as a moon, ice-blue tablecloths that bound up the night tight as a cradle like a mother, indispensible.

I held my skin tight.

The lead poisons that slid over the icy glass, that gave me back myself yellow and taut as a mandarin, made my lover a reptilian opponent.

Yet the wind was right. The tea-leaves spelled something sparse but mercurial. I wandered hourly, nightly, among the starry wastes of a restaurant grown slow as infinity, ringed by a midnight velvet, the golden music stuck to my dress like lametta.

MARIANNE'S SECOND DREAM OF THE ODEON

I once had a lover who glittered like a huge spinning mirror-faceted ballroom globe hanging above me my fragments held by a hair to each particular splinter in his glass heart. We took long indigo walks. The shadows outmaneouvering each other among pines. The crushing of feet, of wishes. The rock formation of her skull where only termites danced and the arms that made a canyon for his wild howl of caged ecstasy. And she, she was all lavender and wreaths.

She pirouetted like a late butterfly among the skull orchard, the bony tables.

Those were pearls that were his eyes.

She plucked the winter berries, the mistletoe.

And the band all pink and satin like an arrangement of lush fruit, struck up another number.

The wind howled among the tubular bells. . . .

Lord said Marianne, I can't keep my head in one place. But she couldn't help comparing Marbles to the slow latin heart of the man from the local bank who had made good and whose demands were secular and made her faint with nostalgia. Instead of this—game of cells, this intrusion of what was not yet come. She longed for her opulent cage. Her carved memorium. She remembered her mother with a sharp pain that was worse than the wind, positively getting at her now. As though Marbles had planned it, weather and all; even the way the grass grew smelt of his hand upon it.

She had the unpleasant feeling that he had taken over the world. Every particle, every blade.

But that was nonsense. That did not make sense. And he, was a man of sense. A man of painstaking relationship. The grass would only be of Marbles if he had grown it. He was mere manure, she the blood that flowed green as vitriol through the flesh-leaves. Spreading my hand over this green breathing field as my own, she thought.

But that didn't answer directions. The message of the north star in daylight. Not a ribbon of sun. Not a wink from the heavens.

An old woman smelling of potatoes— weren't they tumours?—Marbles again, coming up the lane.

THE TREASURE-SEEKER: MARBLES ATTENDING

Marbles regained his cool, the dust and shade of his laboratory, and laid the table for dinner.

He was overburdened oversized in the tubegame, the glass shoot digging for her, knowing the air full of fuzzsound, whine of a torn fly. His words were losing their sense of direction. How had he lost contact?

They swing into the opening bars of the moonlight sonata caught by a dripping tap arteries frozen for this monumental capture, this liquid arabesque.

The sound pours through Marianne like soft-toothed predators, digging out darkness with small claws, ripping silently across all the tubular network (it will wear off in time he said), a maze of glass.

And this, said Marbles, is act the second, my *coup de grâce*, my *pièce de résistance*, my sunshine caught in a bottle. The air seemed to freeze. Marianne pulled up her stockings.

He handed it to her, parchment and pearl-embossed, shorn off from the bone, crackle of the nicest letter she had ever read, violet and soft-smelling, rainbow resurrections. Marbles and tubular bells.

Her aunt was throwing stones at the

radio set. Uncle Jack read the instructions too many times and missed the turning. The sky turning, turning.

I invite you to a sinfonietta, it said,

I invite you to see yourself in my new brass bed.

Marianne said, I will draw a flower on my night dress for your collection of pleasures, remembered not to spell your name as I undress, unpeel, unrealise my silky tarnished skin.

The sun made of wicker.

laminated flax. straw surrogate.

The grass is nervy.

Marbles' laboratory, one degree west.

You failed, said Marbles. I can't hear your story. Marianne gave him the white, unwritten, mother of-pearl sheet, the unsucked breast of her dream.

Write me another letter, he said.

She dreamed crisp lettuce salad, iceminerals, poppy-faces, she ran frantic among the mazes of glassy clues, but she could not find it, could not find them. Where was the key to stop the machinery? Where was the master notebook, the letter many years old, yellow as aunt alice, who presided. His notebook stretching end to end the

length of the room, black, red, white—
where was Aunt Alice? She pulled out a
diary, midnight to one a.m. thursday the
second of march nineteen forty-three. Aunt
Alice was dead then. She left her tablecloth
to Marbles. The tightly-packed pages clung
together against intrusion.

Marbles had covered his sore blue wound.
He set his head at the right angle and was
ringmaster, surgeon, practitioner of other-
people's dreams once again.

While his own worried their bones from
behind cages, hissing from under lizard
stones. He was banking on the blindness of
women set to a task with an end, snapped in
mid-flight, fiery with heads to the stars.
Marianne's knickers were white and wet as
she grappled in head and hands among the
books, among the dials and buttons, trying
to find the treasure. Marbles was a speck at
the other end of the laboratory. The floor
cracked open like lightning. The mud sent
up a fever of mud-sound. The hissing,
bubbling, tubular under-earth closed round
her ankles, and still her eyes skimmed the
high vaults and caverns of air that floated
over Marbles' experiments, gesticulating
antennae of intention.

Proof! bellowed Marbles. You are helpless without my key. She lost the second set, defiant. The tears of the subterranean kingdom could be heard pouring through the faucets.

Clothed and confined, she made her request.

His logical mind could not but accept.

This time, she said, your task is within my landscape.

Marbles laboured a full minute with the abyss, cutting loose. I shall require to remain in full charge of all my faculties, he said.

MARBLES WRITES TO HIS FRIEND CONCERNING TRANSMISSIONS AND AUNT ALICE

Dear Godfrey,

I feel compelled to write to you and describe my totally unexpected condition. I knew that I had left the balcony game behind, but still I am constantly attacked by swarms of white dandelion hairs that remind me of brides. And breakfast is heavy with electrical messages that sing among the cereal and interrupt my poached eggs by infecting the knife and fork with spasms of metallic trembling. The words she let fly are caught in a fine invisible web of static that hangs like a cloud of bluebottles over the marmalade.

I wish these friends—and their director, I suppose it must be her—would be more considerate and allow digestion. The table is an inferno of cross-purposes. Nothing is *clear* Godfrey—I can't find an exact quantification of meaning. I call for an electron, or a truce, but these invisible orators obviously grow fat on the bursts of rage that emanate at intervals from deep in my throat, like puffs of encapsulated flame, mushrooms of crimson energy.

It doesn't matter where I am—in the house, or out walking in the fields. When the mood takes them, I am outwitted by *seeds.* I am laid bare by a mere shiver on the air, the humming of invisible riders, small ships of gleaming discoveries, blueprints wrapped in tiny crystal impulses that inject me with what I can only think of as a liquid so swift it speeds to my heart before I can capture it.

And what is worse, I can't do my work. I spell out the words of the telephone directory to counteract these spells of weightlessness. I've installed radios in my house, turned on night and day. But the many silver buttons are alive with dust and I can only hear other messages—of fire, and the slow blue birth of an alien moon.

I scuttle like an itinerant crab beneath the leather-bound voice that is the unacted sex of my ageing Aunt Alice. Her skirts seem to absorb some of this mercury, this powder that knows each gaping aperture, each entrance, each lobby, each cavity, deserted for centuries. But then Aunt Alice is a large area of inert bones, linked by a wasteland of veins and arteries, hung with flesh stiff as a starched tablecloth for the new monarch, embroidered with initials of someone she has forgotten who never got further than the border.

Yes, she knows how to manage Marianne and her emanations. To enter Aunt Alice's house is to receive the blessing of a cold dank hand, and hear the laughter recede and the tinkling words trail down her flagged path like snails in flight. But I cannot visit Aunt Alice without a tremble in the bones, and the re-echo of gates slotting shut, of a fading sun, and my heart pinned to a plate of bread and butter and thin jam.

So, dear friend, I wage a war here in this few thin feet of dancing cellular disorder. This is my last cry for help, while even now the page opens under the scalpel, splitting into a wound of slow rusty granite, of a green luminous lady who wears thighs like windows (she has many disguises)—and I, struggling to master a structure so that I may transmit to you my distress, am even now seeking that warm green moss which is called her centre, and finding the greatest difficulty constructing this frail bridge of straws to try and reach you, over her opalescent flesh.

Please send me the following—(the noise is rising to a thin silver scream, like a needle sewing distant parts of me together. I must stop it before the threads bind me completely, before I am become a knot, apex of all unheard-of messages)—I need a hammer, a thick blanket—(I can hear stars whisper inside the bedside clock)—a wig of short dark hair—could you manage a set of tubular bells?—I am running out of batteries—a recipe for indigestion, herbs various, tuning fork (perhaps if I unearth the piano?), a beehive (with instructions), a new deck of cards and a rope ladder. But best of all Godfrey, if you could manage a visit? My laboratory has taken a new direction, and you were always a perfect gentleman among vampires. . . .

Your affectionate friend,

Marbles

And Marbles said, let there be something other, than this skull suspended like a lamp in the machinery of nerves, conductor of plasm, cool white beam of knowing that pierces my heart and cuts my room into rectangular segments like a fruit all split, language of refrigeration. Let there be other-than-light which noses into all pockets and folds, all creases, the flight of the world across my retina, the frozen procession of guests probed and explored. . . .

I, said Marbles, am tired of writing the script.

And laid down his pen in an uneasy shiver of his pocket-watch, his potted plant, his underwear hung up to dry.

Somewhere, cavernous, his heart stopped ticking.

Out of the folded, crumpled, room-without-breath, the edges of the woman drawn in fine ink, the thick black border spilled into leather thighs, the belts and buckles of a caught moth, the door opens. All the candles that have sucked that air into their flames lean eastward and expire again.

She leans on one elbow on the mantelpiece of shades and flows to the edges of her armadillo flesh. The cobwebs of marriage float from her metal shoulders. Her cigarette juts from a painted mouth that was the last shape to be added, like aggressive ivy, clinging.

You called? she said.

Marbles didn't know. Had he spoken? He didn't know.

It was a not unpleasant sensation.

I like your jeans, he said. Seeing himself in the polished black laminated curves of Marianne's buttocks. (She was by this time raking her scarlet fingers through his soft shirts, flashing like sudden blood, the careful piles of cream and amber cloth turned and fell, settled and hardened again).

The room was a thin corridor. He had only made room for a small crack, like a rumour. His desk spread itself into the spaces. The warehouse of his room rang with the pushing, heaving mass of unacted dream.

Marianne outlined herself once more against the wall. She was his perfect guest. Marbles was pleased with what had squeezed in between the blinking of his eye. Marbles congratulated himself on the perfect figure of womanhood that he had allowed to enter his matchbox heart.

Marbles felt gratified that what had come between the busy whirring of his pen (an electronic model, newly invented) was such a perfect example of his art. Marbles noticed the glossy surfaces of every part of her, the way each movement was a complete gesture, each draw on the cigarette (that never grew less) performed with the completion of a dancer's speech, the feet in their black leather shoes set at an exact right-angle, the belt a zodiacal masterpiece, eyes with exactly the right measure of crystalline appraisal.

What a collection of parts!

His eyes gleamed in their pale-blue sockets. The veins in his hand registered an unnecessary agitation. Better watch out, she was the best yet. . . .

He lifted his latest creation and lay her stiff, her angles intact, on to the vast windy area that was his bed. Her cigarette flared at one and a half inches and his face flickered in every fleshy crevice.

She will do for my hero's lady-friend, thought Marbles, pleased that he had not had any hand in the construction. He cherished the thought that she had come to him intact—that was true mastery.

He held the figure of black bone between his fingers, turning and turning. He cherished the thought that she came from

the unknown precincts outside his laboratory, turning, turning it, until it lay like a
pebble at the base of his throat. She will do
for my hero's lady-friend, he thought. She
fits me to perfection.

*

Under the armoury of his rattling type-
writer, Marianne's flesh-fingers folded into
his hair, her moth-hands flickered somewhere above his head. She saw how the
light caught and held the edges of his face,
how the air was thick and dense in this
room, with many careful journeys like
hanging cobweb maps for her to choose. In
the encasing shape of her newest womanhood, Marianne's blood seeped slowly from
its dark, unseen, hidden, a quiet river. And
she spread her paper wings that could not
last long and caught the descending sun, the
fiery latticework of light into whose game
she entered. While the stiff, prescribed form
fulfilled many missions on the barren windy
plain that was his bed, she explored the
room's underside, the shadow, the un-
claimed language of her scarred skin, the
flotsam of untidy, greedy tides.

THE GARDEN OF CLOSURE
(AFTER LUNCH)

The words unfold from their closed silence.

My dream pricks, like the distant cactus, said Marianne.

Marbles gave her a brand new mirror.

In the garden, a moth.

In the garden, the arrival of a stranger.

The air is gold and stretched at my side like a wing I have lost, said Marianne. It comes near and settles on the sea-blue blanket at my side, the pale white drift of her sister self alight on the grass.

Marbles gave her the sound of the earth and the anchoring laughter that chained itself to the trees and held her fluttering heart steady.

The light is awash with this luminous visitor, says Marianne. I am here in the held breath between us. I am here held by a mesh of gold and white wires that sing and make patterns over the grass. The words unfold from the tiny white page and are like fingers stroking, the wings of my old messages.

Marbles resonated under her skull.

The dark caverns of her eyes felt his shadow pass.

The deep tolling of his voice reminded her of the geometric night.

The passing of this visitor is all I ask, said Marianne. Breathing the air that shifted. Sorting the coloured clothes.

Her laughter rang from the tips of flowers and she took and gave that luminescence, breathing the gold and blue light deep into the tomb where Marbles lies still, his tail at rest.

I feel the distant tremble among his skins and the slow passage of the plant through its life-spiral, waiting behind the blind curtains, the occasional fruiting.

The garden is alight, said Marbles.

You will burn in that cool fire.

I am only a moth, said Marianne.

Only a moth to be taken.

One wing burned in the afternoon sun.

Marianne vanished between one breath and the next.

She entered the circle, and was gone.

POSTCARD FROM THE TAMAR
BRIDGE, SALTASH

He, the draftsman, now turned to collage.
The subject was a figure he thought he had
once seen in a workshop. A chance combination of machine scraps, a trick of
perspective. This glimpse of order he took to
be a living soul—for the purpose of his
creative work of course—and decided it was
a returning soul, a spirit, a star jongleur at
the game of being. He would turn this trick
into a collage, a framed expression of
mechanical anguish: a wrecked car, torn
buildings, mounds of split concrete, metallic
slabs, flying rivers and shredded leather,
dripping with dismantled flesh. Is all this in
store for your car? he mused. When it was
nearly completed, some features of the
spirit he had originally glimpsed still re-
mained. They somehow didn't seem to fit in
with the rest of his picture, so he covered
them up with a pair of blue eyes and some
items of underwear cut from a magazine.
Now the magnificent horror of his creation
stood slim and sublime before his type-
writer. 'Excellent' he thought, folding
fingers through his hair. He didn't publish
his work. He put it in an empty, unaddressed
envelope, and sent it back to hang in the

workshop. Disguised as a mirror, in the hope that the figure he had once seen was still there, and that she might take it to be a message from someone who couldn't speak her language: or who didn't care to. He pointed every article in the workshop towards this supposed mirror so that they could not avoid its gaze. He blew out a candle, lit another (with the same flame) and failed to notice a moth (attracted to his gauloise) skim his now-deaf ears. It impaled itself on the stubble of his unshaven chin.

KB. Alias Marbles.

MARBLES TO BLACK KNIGHT
(ACCOMPANIED)

Each time I enter this room there is the smell of burnt leaves, the nuptuals of autumn. The walls unlock themselves, and stare at my thin dress, stones overthrown, the mist lifted, bells rung, yet something traces itself on the skin of my hands under the gloves, Marianne said.

Something unseasonal. Remnants of sacrifice.

There is a black cock, chained by one leg to the corner. There is the smell of disinfectant and charred papers. (Are these his unwritten epics or the completion of galaxies reduced to a thin grey powder that will lie small in its urn her face turned towards the great elm having spent her life wishing for language?)

I struggle to remember that my hands belong to me as I enter this room where the light is in perpetual struggle with itself, pushing aside the berries and dreams, the hordes of shadowy guests who are sitting, are hung, who float, who leave and enter eternally (was the small grey woman, with head bent, of Marbles? Marianne saw her, like a snail across the grass, leaving a trail of forlorn leaves) whose bones are piled against the desk, whose smile hangs disembodied above the vast windy plain that is the. . . .

In the chair, he sits. He has no features. He does not speak. His eyes are unwritten, his head like a pendulum refusing to enter time.

He sits on the chair. He has no features. A few pieces of straw escape from his chest.

I will name him, Marianne says. I will button him, Marianne whispers. I will take him and stare into that blue unwinking eye. I will gather his grey hands and press them into my side. I will offer oranges and coconut biscuits, marzipan and flowers. My flowers will spring out into the space and whisper their growing. His massive unspoken forehead gleams dully.

His name is Walter, says Marianne. His round blue eye was a country she did not know.

Your name is Walter and Marbles. I tell you my story, but you were not there. I tell you where I have been, but you have no memory. My stories speed from all parts of me and fill the room with the sound of cities. Do my elaborate dances trouble you? I am soft as a moth.

The black cock is crowing. Books shift uneasily on their shelves. Marianne and her shadow endlessly pirouetting in the centre of the room.

And Marbles' hand, with its mercurial veins, is for a moment made flesh, descends the great tunnel of his extended skull, spirals down his throat, along the veins and arteries of his chest, and reaches the edge of her. There it stops, hangs, holds itself, and moves across the pristine, unresistant flesh, reaches the edge of his journey that writes itself over her skin.

The end of the monster-merchants is his single thought. Then he withdraws.

And Marianne falls into the shadowy area of the black and humming space that is bequeathed her, falls from a great height into the vast jungle of the afternoon sun, thanks him for tea and leaves the room like a good guest should, having touched her perfect host, for a brief moment, by the hand. . . .

ROOMS AND CORRIDORS

There is a stirring in the corridor, like a hand clenching. An iron fist, or the rusty wings of a late moth trying to enter. Along the walls a sensation that was no more than the whispering of summer trying its hand at capture, the uncertain heat that strokes the distant hills like a wife wearing beads as she is waiting.

Not needing a sound to tell her, Marianne lifts her head and listens, to the light making jungles along the window-sills, drawing the murmur of wood and grass and of this month that sees in a new moon's blueprints, into herself, feeling the light, skeleton leaves whispering among her blood.

That footfall, that blueprint, was the arrival, the garden's crucifix, the death of winter. Marianne slowly unhinges the wings of a dead moth that was mutilating her page and puts them into the brown envelope. Yesterday it had battered itself senselessly against her face, as though the life that played there among the bones was a bright flame that would forever give it life. The flame that is blue in the first morning that no one sees, and by mid-day is fierce like a forest-fire.

No, said Marianne, to her portrait of Marbles. You do not know the cool blue flame of my unseen hours. And the silence cracked.

Splinters of the chosen name. Pieces of the moth's life-story brushed carelessly past the glass where a cracked face shone, forever white, forever reflecting.

She would take her time over this metamorphosis. Her notes on Marbles were incomplete.

This once was a single marble. It came and went. Sea-blue statuette of a once-moth entombed in a world of glass. There was a time when these transparent walls were liquid—glowing red and boiling with some unknown fever. Its light drew this moth, traced its shadow on the open walls. Its heat gave it purpose, but took its breath. The mixture cooled, set solid like its sister rock and became symmetrical, a perfect sphere, allowing no possibility of irregularity, no sign of eccentricity to pock its veneer, no weakness in its silk crust which might give hint of escape.

All its sides merge and face inwards. They are silvered so that the inner is reflected. The marble is now opaque. The light inside it bounces around for ever, but from the outside it is a shadow, a dark noose-knot hanging in space. This black hole once was a marble.

This once was many marbles. They came and went.

Ripples skating across them, scattering their osculating forms, alighting nowhere. Seeds stirred in breathless motion, unable to germinate. Each collision threatens disintegration—shattered glass and skidding rocking hemispheres, torn with a death-laugh, setting into the sniggering joy of release from perpetual clattering motion. Outside the tin walls of this clatter the earthbreath tosses. It pushes and prods the rattling box perched on a fleshy monolith, wondering which unearthly stream or trade wind delivered this misericord. A small useless door in its side announces 'no visitors allowed'. No eye is sharp enough to pierce the cracks it leaves. No sense could fathom its rattle. Translucent glass unknown in a tin box, breeding mystery. Around it built a tin scaffold where many cuckoos built nests hiding the flesh monolith until this unusual combination becomes legend. The legend is confused and lost in myth.

The Myth of Marbles—that they were once many.

I hope I've got it right, said Marianne. Been fair to him. Objective.

She had drawn on many sources for her data, particularly KB who arrived at the beginning, but left early.

MARIANNE AND MARBLES:
OF ENTRANCES

Marbles' jacket hurt him. So did his socks. So did his watchstrap and his pocket calculator. So did Marianne's clear blue eye tracing the shape of his tie, his buttons, the seams of his shirt-sleeves. Along his hairline, the unmistakable itching of his name.

I am swinging in the old garden among the fidgety leaves, says Marianne. The garden is full of people but I swing past all their eyes.

Each is a piece of the garden, and I can flow out to all its corners.

Quiet, said Marbles, adjusting his button. The round, amorphous twilight of his head was jerked into sharp focus. He could read there the contents of his evening meal, the conversation with his sister yesterday evening, the map of his route to the west coast next easter, his pulse-rate, the notation of the birdsong on the tree at the bottom right-hand end of the garden, the football results, predictions concerning the state of the american astronaut in four days time, reminders that his tennis racquet needs a new string, and times of the buses to laburnum avenue, where aunt alice kept up the national anthem ceaselessly among marigolds and nasturtiuns.

Your face is unfamiliar, says Marianne. I am watching the games of children in the labyrinth of shadow. Your voice is of the texture of all the soft seasons. The knives that you see are indiarubber children's toys, my words are a filtering network at evening; the space around you is set hard as a steel trap. Silence! roared Marbles, disconnecting the current. The voices ceased. His clothes seemed to have solidified hard to his skin. He removed his jacket like a building-block, his shirt like a shop-window dummy, his hair-oil fell like plastic confetti.

Finally Wednesday's clothes stood before him, a momument to that voice he had tuned into another satellite, a brisk, almost defiant thrust into the chilly air.

That's Wednesday, grumbled Marbles. Its not summer yet. And retired into the central room of his laboratory where no light could enter to speak him and no sound could enter to mould him and no soft song of substantiation. No moth-hands to rumple the perfect symmetry of his hairs.

He smiled. He had outwitted them. The impaled insect was atomised underfoot.

And the presence of the child endlessly swinging was, for the moment, eternally obliterated from his memory.

Until the box, the room, the blanket-dark, the silk-silence, the cautious cushioned hub of his own obliteration, imperceptibly shifted, then rocked, then swung, Marbles and all, out into the unblinking stare of the summer garden, the harsh scraping of the swing carving through the air, the names of plants and trees singing, the gaze of the guests, the touch of all the unseen currents that Marbles had never found, crossing and lacing his path. The pendulum swing of an invitation.

Inside, outside, the dark creases, folds.

Outside the summer hammocks curve into a new shape.

Inside, he could not hear could not see could not define the slightest sensation.

Except that now the darkness seemed to contain a knot, a crust, a slight hardening in the centre of his forehead. It took Marbles some time to realise that this density was linked by a thread to the very centre of his solar plexus. He did nothing, anonymous, nothing. There wasn't the slightest change of air.

But the knot slowly paled, into smoke, into glass. There slowly formed two inches from his forehead a transparent lens through which the garden swung in miniature. It was the clearing of the mirror, set in his neckstone. He had forgotten to take it off. He had forgotten to remove the hanging globe which connected him to the power that had directed him into the box, the voice that in his absence kept the garden going: Aunt Alice, the astronaut, the cabinet-maker, the lens-grinder, Marianne, his personal chorus.

The decision lengthens into afternoon shadows. Something like Marbles flitters among the late flowers and is seen mouthing instructions. But no sound comes. When Marianne reaches out a hand to touch that nebula, there is a falling like cobwebs and the gentle parting of the grasses as the visitors leave unseen.

The waves on that particular afternoon recede, overlapping.

Marianne feels for the chain around her neck.

It has broken. Marbles is missing.

Where is he? Is he caught in her hair like the half-remembered moth whose wings she had stolen? Is he entombed and fossilised into one of his own formulae? Has he fallen into the spaces between the names that are the aunts and uncles and cousins, the companions whose lives he rides like a scavenger? Is he lost in one of his messages?

Without Marbles, the garden is awash with her tears. She searches her handbag for all the marble postcards, tiny fragments of sound, the half-hidden wishes, the notebooks of entry, the chilly sculptured words falling like pebbles from her fingers, as she digs deep into the blue spiral that is Marbles, the blue curling flame deep at his root, the singing humming garden growing nearer and more brilliant until it breaks in a great flood, scattering words, nails, rope and lattice, her balustrades of freedom.

OF MARIANNE'S FRIEND,
NOT YET COME

She lay very still and let the swirling moments settle.

She lay at the hub of afternoons of lazy power.

Working hard, Marianne managed to part the filter that was the web and tapestry of wall and flower and green sap, and saw glinting there the shadow of something dark that had come all unexpected into the hidden hours and now filled her head with a joyous shadow as though the garden was easily reached by a short walk instead of now as it was pressed between the tight folded papers of memory.

The space that she managed with all her concentration to discover among the stems that would keep moving proved above all that departure had not taken place. There was the uneasy presence of that nocturnal pact among holy ruins shivering in this noonday, infinitely gentle explosion. And in that crack, that rent, something whispered that was not quite of dream (though that promise, that shift in the moment's breath, was all out of bounds) making its presence felt although the sun made the garden quite bare and exposed, she saw in the absolute glare that a kind of antithesis brooded, as though the light gone far enough would fall into its black brother.

The books were piled up against a tree. She slept as though cursed in her old cane chair, the wind a nocturne in the few trees, the birds very still as it came to the heart of the day, the shadow that had promised lay very still against the flat earth.

MARBLES SPEAKS

Marbles spoke, and there was a great space carved out by sound as though the centre of the room had cracked and opened to the unfolding of what it was he was reaching for (she could not see) as the words stretched and curled and eluded him finally until on the periphery of naming he hung like a nerve trying to catch the solid centre of it, and the shapes and colours of his intention danced on the borders of his skull itching to the tune of someone he had caught sight of in last night's negotiations, grown sleepy with waiting for its incarnation.

Marbles spoke, and the toy soldiers of infancy aimed their bayonets and fired pellets into her head.

Marbles spoke, and she was wrapped as though in a shroud of thin linen that breathed in a parallel rhythm to her own skin and was Marbles' shirt, soft and cold, holding her.

Marbles spoke. He made her a new face with his words.

Her mouth wore lips of letters shaped like themselves. Marbles spoke. Marbles needed a name.

In that hinterland that was the only landscape she knew, was the scurrying flashing flickering multiple sound of all possible voices and somewhere there was her own small movement (something to choose perhaps among the crowd) that tried for the surface and could not break its crust, only hammering at the iron ceiling of the world and succeeding in scratching a name occasionally in the resistant materials that hung always near, veil-like and amorphous as they were, yet taut as metal—only he was looking for names, large red names, capital names that would glare and reassure him, marble names breathing into eternity;

And he did not see hers, soft as feathers among the grasses, the stems of things, somewhere down there (for she did not see them) where plants spring forth and took hold of the air and crept and hid and could not be seen entirely in that hinterland that was the only landscape she knew, essentially of shadow with some of the letters missing.

He could not see that broken landscape, where the paths meet and the petal breaks from its host nebula. Where the uneasy silence of no name sends forth its edges into the infinite circle of light spreading and filtering among the leaves. Marbles stood at the edge of the garden, looking for her. His best yet.

Marbles spoke, and the sound that spilled out of his mouth was like a mirror breaking.

THE HINTERLAND AND
MARIANNE'S ROOM

In the hinterland that was the only landscape she knew, Marianne took on the
opponent and left aside the backcloth that
was the this and that, the hanging of
curtains long or short, the meal at six or
seven, a blue or a brown shirt, first the fire
or the table, the clamour of vase or flower,
garden or concrete, bread and book, broke
like a wave that left her slowly, receded,
until she stood on the sandy wasteland
alone, with the protagonist the steely one,
against whose iron tongue she must temper
her own voice, which even now haunted the
shadows beneath the tablelegs, under
shelves, among the folds of clothes and
crumpled papers, the hanging canopies
between one mealtime and the next, when
the choice, the decision would thrust a
starfish, a fragment of wood or broken glass
on to that pristine seashore.

And it would not matter. That was not
the point. Should the meal be this week or
next, would it be long or short the curtain
(that question hung even now on the
borders of her symmetry, as the gathering
took place and she travelled carefully towards the centre where there waited for her
only the one protagonist always ready) or
should it be done now, today, or later at

some unspecified time. No, that was the very background of it, against which the shadows flickered. Those shadows that even now took root and increased in density until the stuff of them was already present having arrived from a great distance with all the flesh and bone and cloth arranged in the patterns necessary for it.

No, she did not look at Marbles. Instead she folded her head of rags and laid it upon the pillow in the white room reserved for such a truce.

It could wait until tomorrow.

And she let the shadows out of the door, like the last party guests, until the house was quiet again and the old brown table could wait in its own way to be released and the sharp edges could blur a little and the wind that was trying to get in at the bedroom window could murmur all by itself without her help.

Side by side, each took a pillow, a blanket, a corner, a slice of the dark and would sleep (in a while when the air settles) each with his own house intact, just the edges not quite clear, overlapping here and there like the interlacing of fingers now and then during this long night.

MARIANNE'S MOON-DANCE
(MARBLES ATTENDING)

Marianne felt the light pressing as against a web on the other side of consciousness, felt it dribble and spill and tiny fragments of the day breaking in across concrete yards, through blades of grass that were like spears to autumn, cutting across the tiny chasms that held her apart, hovering over the old brown table (recently found) and the white china.

Marbles sent her a postcard that was all in ruins.

And in the middle a house, strong and dark and holding firm to its root.

Marbles brushed aside the facsimile of Marianne that dashed itself against his retina. This moth that sought its candle was like gravel caught against his eyeball. The image made a veil as of moonlight over his instrument. And it was mid-day. The earth was red.

Marbles looked at a sample of blood. The lace after-image of Marianne's split-second arrival made it seem that the earth was torn by a veil, caught in a moment's flood before the clock struck twelve and she was banished to that distant shore picking the dead starfish.

Holding his metal tube cold as the north star, Marbles gazes down into the heart of blood seeing the tides rise and fall.

This mirror had caught her face. Here it was held between the shoreline of cells that nervously quivered at their edges.

As a mirror reflects a life, Marbles' stone drew itself back and the surface began to dissolve. Holding an apple and an axe, Marianne began her slow dance on the seashore, red as coral.

Marbles drew back, turned off his microscope. Unbuttoned his shirt, looked for a towel. Mopped the tears that his skin sent forth for the storm that was brewing under those lids.

And the stones are wild, said Marianne. She broke open a grey sea-bone.

And the piles of them held within themselves the light of all past moons that now stretched out and would burst the skins of the stones. The mass of rock and sand reached towards her as human form and hers was the red rock, the jewel, the eye, tight in the stone's hollow until this moment when Marianne took and held the scarlet blood-stone that shone that glowed, that must be shown to someone who had not yet come, stroking the oval cavity where the stone had laid. These and all the messages Marianne gathered. Soon the washed sea-gleam, the gritty stars, fell from his eyes like tired tears, and the shore closed on itself as each wave hissed and sucked, trying to reach him.

Under those lids, a wilderness of weeds and anemones.

Marianne, her stone, fragments departing, winking out.

Marbles could see only stars, his guests.

Marbles could only see the space she had made on the shoreline, the shadowy tunnel that was left behind her, hands clenched on some starfish or other. It was as though that moment fossilised under his microscope, endlessly.

She would take the stone (unknown to him) to someone who had not yet come, unveiling it, so that it flashed its fierce red fire, an egg dropped from the moon, an accretion of sea-rust, a sea-berry, and he would see and be glad and would watch her dance on the frozen sand with an apple and an axe and the stone in her forehead red and sweet as pomegranate, thick as wax, the marble sand carved by her feet dancing.

And he, able to see, aiming his polished lens westwards, catching the neck and the bone and the intricacies of blood pouring . . . scars and sea-holly, the brute wave. . . .

THE VISITOR

And Marbles said, my laboratory is a
grove of fine sons who will talk in my
many voices and make a red hunting
chorus for me.

Marianne watched the sun leaking under
the kitchen door and wondered if it would
work. At the other end of the telephone Joe
was talking about money.

I'll pay for you, he said, and she hitched up
her skirt and tried to pull up the zip with one
hand.

She thought of the sun. She thought of a
warm cloying heat. She thought of Marbles
but not very hard.

Would he find out?

I'll only have to work one morning, said
Joe. And she thought of the sea and tough
grass and not many people at this time of
year. The sun entering the kitchen. All right
I'll come, she said. I'll find out the times of
the trains.

*

I must close it down, she said, the torn rags
of that summer cliff, that other time, the
sand itching in her hair. All over the place
tiny pieces of laughter rang and tapped at
the glassy day. They had swum and they had
dropped pebbles over the cliff-face. But, said

Marianne, I must close my avaricious mouth and swallow the dream that flies past my eyes. That other time, hanging like a moth. She searches for the reason why this particular air encloses, embraces.

Why did the sun rich on the window come rustily to her side as though it were an old cat, well used to sleep.

Why did the green creased shirt hang on him like a badly-fitting curtain matching the old green socks and all the summer's undersides (and all of summer's murder piled up and facing her like a chorus of tired relatives wanting visiting, wanting a post-card please from the land of plenty).

The train had been late. He had greeted her untidily, spending a few minutes explor-ing the distances—then hurried off to complete his work for that day. She had felt the sinking sun strike at the edge of the hill, and knowing the house from before, made her way to the room which was all tidy and smoothed for her coming.

In the garden, a few chickens. Next door, young boys and a swing.

Now he was sitting splayed across the bed like a seated ballerina so as to come one inch closer, his thighs gaping wide, his brows lowered like rock, seeing it seemed his own powerful image stretched over her face. She felt as though she were lying beneath a net. And his rolling backside thrust out behind him like a pretty girl and eyes full of posturing, and his green plastic shoes, and the garden, waiting for her kiss. Only she could not move under the net. Could not escape this man's self-parody, being his unwilling audience.

But it was only a moment. Suspect. He had reached behind her for his jacket and then plugged in the kettle.

Want some tea? he said. The cups rattled. Unbearable sound, and heavy liquid thick as the soil. She turned on her side and watched him pour the milk bluish and thin (there was a white gauze curtain which gave the room a pale thin film, like white dust). She watched the ritual of the tea-leaves and the mugs and the taut tired air that enclosed them would not break its hold. Little white specks on the surface.

Inside, the petal curled, making a dark place full of soft sounds.

She sipped the tea. It was thin and scented. Not thick at all. She liked it.

She could feel the small curved petal, brushing lightly her cheek, the crabbed fingers, the ache.

Bees humming in the netted windows. White and cream roses thrusting out of the shade. Like a dry plate under the sky, the garden waits humming very quietly as its breath is all gone.

Flat, on the bed, she had shrunk as far as she could into the pillow watching the tea make stains on her blouse, watching the room crack, silence as armour.

And here he was again, absently gathering her skin between pinched fingers.

She shivered.

Not too hard, she said.

A gesture that was no more of love than the lifelong nervous tic inherited from childhood. Under the kneading fingers she lay trying to gather herself.

Its so good to see you, he said, very quiet. The delicate feet of a daddy-long-legs danced over his face.

Long way to come, she said. That flimsy beauty hidden, ever closed on itself, under the weight the self-importance of that leg, those buttocks, those shoulders aggressively squared (they would flex occasionally making the old green shirt flap like a worn out victory flag), that freezing of the room as he came near.

And she. Light as frost. Grown pale now. Grown thin. She, what he waited for. Full of cliff-dreams.

She folded, waiting for it to fade. Waiting

for the bruising thigh to detach itself from her side. Waiting for the stubbed busy fingers to grow tired and be still. Waiting for the words to build into towers of anger.

But not yet. She thought of the moment when she had decided, holding the phone, thinking of Marbles, pulling at her skirt, deciding futures for herself. Cutting roads.

Now, just a flickering irritation like the senseless effort of a late moth. That the garden was beautiful, that there was the sea and the sun.

Marianne waited beneath the touch of this person called Joe, this room that lay wide and open to the sun, in her duplicity and in his, and wished for Marbles to rescue her. Wishes for one of his lectures. One of his potions. For a formula to bring her some blessed relief from the rest of the day and its intrusion.

Joe, all unaware of her frailty, (and would not know how, in what way, with what gesture, to undo it) raked her with fingers that were senseless and knocked at her silence until even the child next door might hear splinters falling and lay like the weight of last time's tides sprawled on this Marianne until she lay brown and crushed and gave off a scent of dying gardens that lay near shores threatened by the salt sea.

I thought we could eat out, said Joe, and her tight throat gave a little.

Marianne felt revenge gathering. With words waiting on the horizon for the particular cornfield to receive them, as they sat with their picnic food under an elm, eating ham and buttered bread and oranges. Then would the words gather and let fall. That'll be fine, said Marianne, as the first shadows fell into the garden, on to the steps, and they walked quite close and slightly out of step, into the streets that were still hot, still warm from the long day's sun.

Their irritation spread over the grained table.

Do you know why you failed your scholarship, said Marianne. She knew the answers. She knew his knowing but he did not know hers. She also knew in the evening light that gave off such things like fireworks that he did not want her there. Did not want her voice, her quick eye, that flicked all over and in and out of his simple building blocks, his castles, his monuments, shapes in the sand.

There's something odd about it, Joe said. They say I'm not suitable. They recommend a craft course, something more practical.

Don't you think there might be something in what they say? She had always thought he had a false image of his work. There was a kind of low thunder where they sat. She could have stayed quiet. Played with the scarlet serviette, let the meal and its slow steam engulf her. Sink into the dilute second journey that offered her such a jaundiced face. Could have left it be. Let the light web of memory rest and the flies chase each other in and out of the curtain. Let her own silence and the interlocking of light be enough. And a kind of physical half-sleep. She could have distanced him. But the lie was there. The pose. The inauthentic shape at her side and within, breathed itself into her pores, and the twin man torn in himself wagged over the table, his two heads grimacing, the one smaller and pale, the great head of his own conceit miming the words, rehearsing his taking of her, pushing the other under and Marianne with it.

Voices cracked and echoed inside Marianne's skull. A girl came and lit the candle. It did not soothe her. She did not see her own lie, his sister.

Why are you so eager to become something you're not, she asked. The way things inside her head were beginning to boil alarmed her. What did it matter that he thought that way. It wasn't her job to ferret about in his life among the leavings, looking for the cultured pearl she wasn't going to find. Sniffing out mistakes.

I'm not going to take any notice of them, Joe said.

Yet her nerves were raw. And the room seemed full of the irritant flies as night came on steadily, with a sudden flicker of lust as his image flashed, years old, into her head. There were poppies in the cornfield. Poppies of blood and thunder. The corn yellow as new summer skirts. Floating over the field in small murderous outcrops of sound, words mounting and falling, rocking in the light wind, blown like tumbleweed.

Ages ago, Marianne said. You might have listened.

What was a reasonable length of time, he said.

Is just as long as I need, Marianne said.

Ridiculous in this heat-haze, the shimmering mirage of a picnic with apples and pears and warm cheese and hot thick bread.

Torn clothes.

A room with no future.

Faces that faced summer like a green-eyed

doll. Unknown to her, as they ate in silence, his edgy heart prepared its alibis, an unmistakable smell of burning. The next day lay ready to receive her absence. She could see dark ribbons of sweat down the bodice of her dress. She could see how her skin raged under him. She could see a butterfly, all that was left, hunting.

They had finished the goulash, and he asked her for some fruit. He lit her cigarette from the candle. She could see how he would never know her, not in one small particle. Only her sisterhood, her toy-future.

She remembered her old brown doll, and the garden fence. She said, I turn my head upon this particular stalk in this minute of time that hangs between one journey and the next (except that one) and there is no duplicity and there is no twin neck and the marks that I make on the air will not come again and when I lay on that sheet and the pillow at that particular angle with the light just turning between one degree of shadow and the next and open myself all blown and brown like the flower ending, there is no repetition.

It is just like this.

Take longer to satisfy, he said.

And no remembrance.

She stubbed out her cigarette and watched him pay for the meal.

And as I leave this small burning station and as I fall from the train with the grey concrete rising up to meet me, and as the stars of this coast come out one by one and as the river silently swims into my head that is hot and troubled as that one hunting butterfly missing its scent, your life clamps itself to my flesh.

Would you like a walk through the town, he said.

You tighten the straps on my wrists and ankles and lead me through this small fishing town, that I loved in the summer with its boats and wide waters.

It seems just the same, Marianne said.

And turn on the current and pinned as I am to the vast windy area that is your bed, I undertake the requisite movements, the correct proportion of ecstatic gestures. And lay my fingers on that inert back and be comfortable still and glad to be here and accompany you back from your victory until the blood quietens.

They watched a small parade of lights across the bay.

I live near the sea, said Marianne, but it's not the same.

And get up quietly from the tangled linen and enter the shade and silver light briefly touching the falling roses and the creamy curtain like a web, knowing the earth sure underfoot, calm my enraged and inert flesh, stroke it as a midwife should.

Something to do with age, your body changes, Joe said.

That which I am I give to this place, said Marianne. Back in the nursery a doll sighed. Only that was already gone. On that day, he had thrown bread to the birds, staring at the cloud of her that was lavender and wore flesh. Did he not know the workings of such creatures as she lashed at him among the queen corn, the inner space of her twisted like a huge spiral screw, years she had known marked by the flags of a manikin's expeditions?

Her scream tore the earth with the very shape of his entry. And his knife carved the name that was to bind them to this strip of pale gold land specked with the blood of poppies. For as she cast him off, her body filled up with summer. The earth fell and thudded under her heels.

He had risen. He had killed.

Her flight across the land made water run from his brittle eyes.

Instruments. Small broken things. He picked up the banana and orange peel and carefully piled the picnic litter into a heap, opened a paper bag and put it all in, took the tablecloth and folded it.

I'll take you back where you belong, he said.

Marianne laughed, remembering, curled upon herself. And knew that it was Marbles.

REQUIEM

His face for a moment in the square glass pane of the lorry cab. As I hurry elsewhere, says Marianne. As the face turns and spirals through the corridors of my bones, that remember.

The dream subsides. Said Marbles. Said Marianne.

And the next week, in Sydney Street, the clothes hung like dead moths on their window hooks.

And Marbles said, my laboratory is a grove of fine sons who will talk in my many voices and make a red hunting chorus for me.

Between you and me and the moths and the crickets and the goat, I want to go home, said Marianne (seeing nothing but red)

And slid from under his wing.

What! Leave this game of consequences with its red faces and its grove of new songs, said Marbles, leading her into the red and brimming room where eyes hovered and words dripped from the walls.

A moth drowned in the wastepipe. Marbles in his red shirt, (one button missing) computing unknown jungles, lakes and groves, in moonlight.

It is a red month, says Marianne. I hunt at dawn in a grove of daughters, silent as the knife that dips and seeks the root.

And so she slept.

Over the hills, the ticking of one heart; the grove of small trees stained red, the sounding of names, came and went in their dream. . . .

This novel, or romance, grew directly out of my work in philosophy, at the same time bringing to an imaginative level and in a new form, what I see as the male-female dialectic, which may also be seen as the apparent dichotomy of various ways of being-in-the-world.

For example, Marbles, as his name suggests, is polished, round, defined, completed, unresistant; while Marianne is soft, pliable, resilient, amorphous. Thus on a purely tactile or sensual level, the two are juxtaposed.

Marbles organises, Marianne allows organisation.

Marbles may be said to represent the position of the scientist-rationalist, the logical-positivist, a man who relies for his safety upon a logical construct of the world, seeing it, as it were, in the mechanistic view as an aggregate of parts. While Marianne may be said to represent the magus, the spell-maker, who allows the world's own contribution to enter her manipulations. Thus freedom for her is not absolute, but means working with the inevitable. She is witch, existentialist, and for her the world is and organic whole. She is the moth, the particular, the sensual. For her, the world is not a well-organised machine, but a labyrinth of sensual delight.

Marbles and Marianne are not 'symbols-of' aspects of the world, but are respectively operational-in the world, which they themselves structure in different ways. They are agents of the mode of being-in-the-world that they represent. The importance of their interconnection lies in their interdependence. They are locked in mortal combat and cannot do without each other. Marbles has Marianne as subject-matter for his experiments (even as the critic needs the novel, poem, painting) and Marianne needs Marbles to make sense of her world, to order it and to bring it to consciousness.

Marbles-and-Marianne is an androgynous being, endlessly manipulating its own forces, powers and desires.

*

The novel is about control, competition. The male-female dialectic, totalities and particulars. Of consciousness and science.

Marbles and Marianne—which contains the other?

*

The romance is a journey from the abstract and the symbolic to the concrete—the actuality and the flesh.

The novel is essentially about domination —epistemological, conceptual, sexual. Not of man over woman (though that may be here also), but of that which is blind to its own alternatives, *over* those alternatives.

Domination occurs through one's mode of being in the world, the way in which one structures the world. And also the language which one uses to structure the world is itself a form of domination. (Social structure may well be the prime factor here, in which case the protagonists may represent collective organisations).

Here is a labyrinth of encounter, the domination of the whole by the part, (personal, and/or social).

*

'The Visit' at the end, is Marianne's attempt to escape from her enslaving male archetype—or her flesh and blood father if preferred—into a real-life, normal relationship, and her failure to do so. This represents a movement into concrete subjectivity for the female, her attempt to dance the moondance for herself, rather than for the man. But she cannot escape. Nor can any woman escape from relationship to men finally. This is part of the resolution of the issue—that the mutual dependence of male and female cannot be escaped from, only accepted and transcended.

Each is enslaved by the other only while each envies the other, and while trying to incorporate *all* of the other into the self.